PARTY!!

BE Fabulous ☆

NO BEASTS↓

PIGS

NO SNAKES

NO CAMELS

The BEASTLY BUNCH

Leisa
Stewart-Sharpe

Pippa Curnick

Lemurs

PUFFIN

For the Stewarts, the original Beastly Bunch
L.S.S.

For all the children at Ashby Willesley Primary School
P.C.

PUFFIN BOOKS
UK | USA | Canada | Ireland | Australia | India | New Zealand | South Africa
Puffin Books is part of the Penguin Random House group of companies
whose addresses can be found at global.penguinrandomhouse.com.

www.penguin.co.uk   www.puffin.co.uk   www.ladybird.co.uk

First published 2022. This edition published 2023
001
Text copyright © Leisa Stewart-Sharpe, 2022
Illustrations copyright © Pippa Curnick, 2022
The moral right of the author and illustrator has been asserted
Made and printed in China

The authorized representative in the EEA is Penguin Random House Ireland,
Morrison Chambers, 32 Nassau Street, Dublin D02 YH68

A CIP catalogue record for this book is available from the British Library
ISBN: 978–0–241–64233–7

All correspondence to:
Puffin Books, Penguin Random House Children's
One Embassy Gardens, 8 Viaduct Gardens, London SW11 7BW

Flo was **fabulous** – from the tips of her feathers
to her pink tippy-toes. And **most fabulous** of all
were her parties. *Everyone* wanted an invitation.

There was no better party spot than Flo's house.

The flamingo fountain **sparkled**,
the swimming pool was an **oasis** . . .

KEEP OFF
THE
GRASS

and the fence was *just* tall and pointy enough to keep unwanted guests **out**. Because the *only* thing that wasn't perfect in Flo's pink paradise was . . .

KEEP OFF THE GRASS

. . . her neighbours – the Beastly Bunch.
Flo only had to *look* at them to know they'd be . . .

BITEY,

SMELLY,

SPITTY

AND DIRTY.

So they **weren't** invited. And **that** was **that**.

Instead, Flo only mingled with **cute** and **clever** creatures.
After all, she'd decided *this* party would be her most perfect party yet.
She'd fine-tuned every detail right down to the waiters!

Flo tapped her glass – **TING, TING, TING!**
"Welcome to another perfect party by *moi*," she trilled.
"Now, a party isn't a party without rules, so no misbehaving
and do have a *fabulous* time."

RULES
NO CRUMBS
NO CHATTING
NO SLURPING
NO DANCING
NO SUDDEN
MOVEMENTS
NO POLKA DOTS

Flo flounced across the patio.
"Yoo-hoo, chameleons!
Could you be darlings and change
colour to match the flowers?"

Next, she quizzed the owls.
"Tu-whit tu-whoo,
wise owls. Tell me, what *was*
the largest dinosaur?"
The owls sighed. "We've been
trying to tell yoooooooou,
we're really not that . . ."

But Flo was already halfway across the
garden, gabbling at the penguins.
"Hurry along – the sandwiches
won't serve themselves!"

Flo's guests were *trying* to have a fabulous time. But the only beat was the

PLING PLONG PLING PLONG TWANG

from the harp. And when the animals went for a swim
Flo helpfully reminded them of the rules . . .

"NO SPLASHING PLEASE!"

A snout snorted over the fence.

"Flo-o, we made a cake! Mind if we trot on over?"

"Eww! SHOO, you **beastly** thing!" Flo shrieked.

The snout . . . drooped.

On the other side of the fence, the Beastly Bunch
had finally heard enough.

"I've had it with that fancy flamingo and her perfect parties,"
Camel bellowed. "Let's throw our own Beastly Bash!"

Pig cranked up the tunes, while Snake blew up balloons.

And in the time it took to say "DISCO"...

the Beastly Bash was pumping!

The low **BOOM-BAM-A-LAM-A** beat made the fence wobble and the penguins

waggle.

And an irresistible smell wafted on the breeze.

"Excuuuuuuse me," the owls called.
"Whooooo's invited to *your* party?"
"EVERYONE!" Skunk beamed.

So, one by one, Flo's fabulous
guests **slipped** under,
squeezed through and
clambered over the fence.

After a glorious few minutes straightening the deckchairs,
Flo pranced across the patio, only to discover . . .

her guests had gone . . .

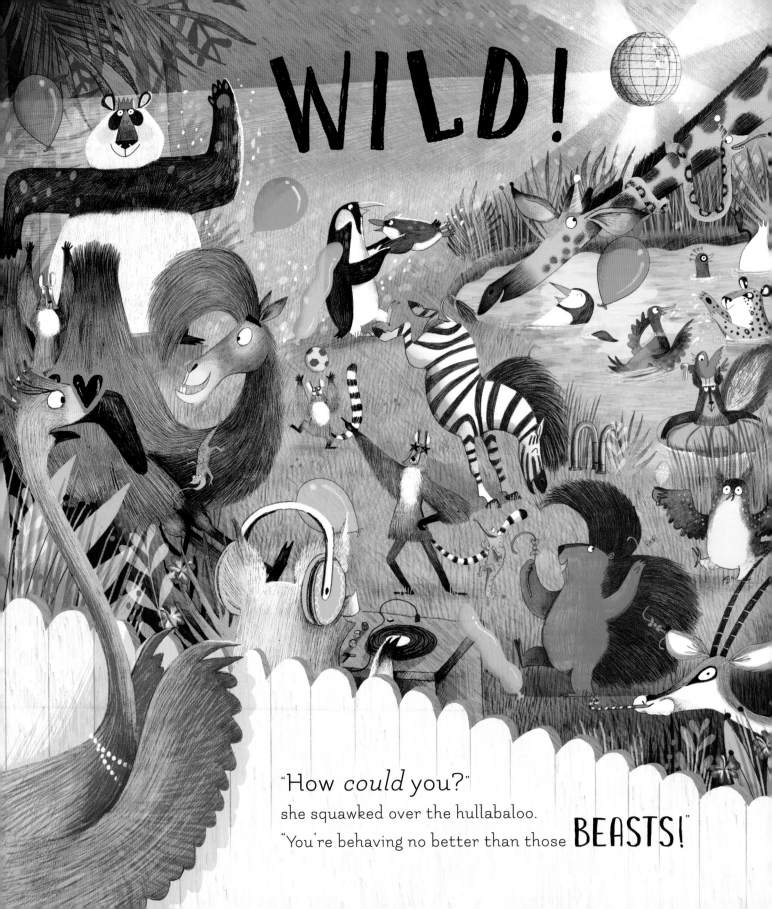

WILD!

"How *could* you?"
she squawked over the hullabaloo.
"You're behaving no better than those BEASTS!"

The Beastly Bash stopped.
Everyone glared at Flo.

The penguins snapped, "They're **not** beasts and we're **not** waiters!"
The owls scowled. "We're **not** wise – just the same birdbrains as everyone else."
And the chameleons glowed. "We **don't** change colour to be fancy.
We go red when we're **unhappy**."

Flo's perfect party was a flop.

Everyone was having a fabulous time next door.

Everyone except Flo.
She'd never noticed that she made her friends unhappy.
If she was wrong about her friends, was she wrong about
the Beastly Bunch too?

Flo knew what she had to do.

She flew over the fence . . .

and on to an inflatable crocodile.

(She hoped it was inflatable.)

"Excuse me, beasts, I mean . . . FRIENDS," she trembled.
"I thought I knew everything about you just by *looking* at you.
But now I see I never really got to know you at all."

A tear slid down her fabulous cheek.

"Truth is, I'm not even fabulous . . .
Without my algae smoothies, I'm really rather drab.
So I just wanted to say . . . SORRY."

Snake slid over . . .

he opened his mouth . . .

stuck out his fangs . . .

And everyone jumped into the pool!

Flo **honked** with laughter.

Skunk smiled. "I just know we're going to be **best friends**."
And he was **right**.

From then on, the Beastly Bunch became Flo's Besty Bunch.
Because, as it turns out, *really* getting to know your friends,
no matter how they look . . .

. . . is BEASTLY fun!

FLAMINGOS turn pink from the algae they eat. (And they LOVE to DANCE)

PIGS roll in mud to cool down.

CHAMELEONS change colour to show their feelings.

SKUNKS switch on "stink mode" when they're scared.

PENGUINS love TOBOGGANING!

SNAKES can swim!

CAMELS spit to surprise!

OWLS throw up their leftovers!